SEEING OCEAN ARDOR BLUES

KASEY C. JONES

authorHOUSE®

AuthorHouse™
1663 Liberty Drive
Bloomington, IN 47403
www.authorhouse.com
Phone: 833-262-8899

Published by AuthorHouse 06/02/2021

ISBN: 978-1-6655-2790-3 (sc)
ISBN: 978-1-6655-2789-7 (e)

Library of Congress Control Number: 2021911350

Print information available on the last page.

This book is printed on acid-free paper.

Dedicated to the family that I started with,
and to the family that I have collected.

Crickets

The crickets sing to me.
They stand behind the river.
They stand behind the riverbed,
singing to me, all the while,
their green voices exude brilliance and rainbows.
The crickets sing to me loud and clear, "I love you
my dear friend, you are the reason I go on."
The crickets sing to me from beginning until end,
and I laugh,
and I speak,
and I laugh,
and I speak,
and I laugh again,
and I speak once more, and I say,
I will not be a tire laying on a fence,
I will not be a ball in the dirt,
I will not be a twig on the ground,
I will not be a feather in a web,
I will not be an acorn flat on a leaf,
I will be, whoever I want to be, so let the cricket's sing.

I Am the Flying Golf Ball

I am the flying golf ball, going to page my journeys addressing
the moment as I propel through the air, flying golf ball will feed
and hover as I plot my work that prevents you, delicacy from getting away.
I would like to be more than happy to land in you, taking sweet trophies
(but really, nothing) in exchange for some suggestive grand stories.
I am a multicolored, white ball of rapid flight with a long
beak sitting on the tracks of your leg as I contemplate first rift
from variegated trees in Central America to refined
places beneath my oh so bleak birthplace of Rosemary, Newsome.
I am a flying golf ball enjoying the lush flashes of (ball) sight,
Honduras, Guatemala and Nicaragua to name just a few.

Although, I have dents in my body I am hard and firm so that

the thieves lurking Sagittarius Rising do not run amuck.
They like to use twigs for poking things that are better than their kind.

Yes, they are also simply insects, found everywhere on each of

my journeys. Always there, to lure me in, to grab my tooth or beak.

They are too my signature, my hair follicle and something in between.

I Will Not be Afraid of The Wind

I will not be afraid of the wind,
no, I will not.

The wind is my friend,
the wind is my friend,
no, I will not be afraid of the wind.
The wind has brought me through
tens of decades,
the wind is a friend to oranges, grapes, hens and humans.
No, I will not be afraid of the wind
my dear friend, no, no, no.
You cannot stop me; you are my friend. You cannot
stop me,
you may not be my friend. Why would I let you stop me?
Why, why, why? I am not afraid of the wind.
Let June ooze from May, let July breeze by and into the
socket with August, and September, I will be consuming
an avalanche.

Part 2

If in the past I feared the wind,
I should have fixed my sleep and
accepted that diving with a broken leg
may only work for fairies.
If in the past I feared the wind,
I must note, I was raised by the desert and
cacti did the best they could with limited water.
If in the past I feared the wind,
Zeus and Hera favored war over hugs, I am sure of it.
If in the past I feared the wind,
in my stinginess I cared for and believed
only the roman numerals.

Please do not worry, I am free of the wind.

Part 3

Please do not worry, I am free,
I am not drowsy, and I am not brainwashed
with any conspiracy theories.
Please do not worry, I am free,
I am paying my own bills and
doing successful adult things.
Please do not worry, I am free
I hug my kids extra to make up for that lack.
Please do not worry, I am free,
I have a passion for learning
what I want and not from a textbook or curriculum.

Have patience you will be exemplary.

Regal Like

Regal like myself, my brother
and sister.

Regal like shading medium,
large and small trees.

Regal like breath mints, "yes
and thank you."

It is midsummer, the magical cattle
encases me, the humming tiger
bird as thousands of us torch the grass with our
stampeding feet.

Out of our comfort zone and into
the wilderness, this regal like bird.

This regal like bird blessing the
land while accepting blessings "yes
and thank you."

Part 2

I can hear you splitting and
Mashing against my teeth,
You, delicious slice of pizza.

You are not regal like the nourishment
I would consume in my kingdom,
but stand aside London, Los Angeles and Ibiza.

Long Nursing Poem

With the people we love, our tenderness
looks ancient yet smeared with
the future and I bathe the
vindicated gook off our arms and legs.
Our tenderness might just be circular and wintry
style of cunning, perhaps beautiful and needed as
opposed to a hideous long nursing poem.

Bricks A.K.A.

For pure pleasure:
No malingerer will keep using my biceps
to combat other people's heads,
I give conditions pummeling through me first,
inspired by vintage wine,
pressured by only the demand of my gloves.
Usually is the plight, might
a young family bruised by such turbulence,
and their politics, and with
our terrorizing enemies cascading thick bricks.
No malingerer will offer my inferences upon
understanding foreign nations pasts therein,
I take initiative to
view myself with their eyes, challenging the Sad.

Vector Field, Fall Thirty Feet

I do not remember the falling, just the over; turning,
that is all.
I recall the black seeping up to me with perhaps an
Angel's lead.
I wasn't Poppin' bottles, shot on pills; or mad drinking
real raw. (But I held the brief scare,
the eminent nothingness I
pushed with my shoes and received fast refuse.)
I'd saw tomorrow smiling in much more before my
young nosey feet.
I will not revisit it because this mind construed a wall
too tall.
I suspect for a blank formation to pass thirty years.
It says nothing except hidden pains,
I wrote it, I moved there without a cause seat.
It shows,
I could fall upon prayer and still walk in God.
I could fall thirty feet and gain wealth, to sob.
I could fall directed by law and wreck on dot.
And marks that
I am the man who will now supersede.
I am the man who will now stand potent.

Bright

Everybody owns their uniqueness
as nature judges being
all I just knew was me.
A single hug or a kiss,
every kind reach kept me here.
I love you, you take me dear.
I wish I could talk to you,
I miss you for lifting me.
The minute you smile at me,
It's known your sincerity,
above mountains are you truly.
All I ever had was firm.
Each deep word gained celerity,
I still keep the light created behind.
I wait eager to be with you.

At the Pier

I see through you internally
like an x-ray, a doctor's viewing,
so pure and trustworthy for me,
with good intentions a mere guest,
on best grounds, up here, beautiful
My enamoring, modest charm.
You attain a lump spectrum of
qualities I wonder, a hue
reflection of a sun we miss,
at the pier, I dream new day.
I fly the path of my own, near the
Cliff, in all my glory for the next.

Roll Reefer

I think God would Roll Reefer
and tie the aircrafts with pure powder
moated
within blue ever from the poplar
and might It to sluice the decks athwart
high,
Its tears the sinews about a stone-
cast when either gusty or at a fire crust
fly.
I think Very low grange upon the
middle of Our Heaven that is blackest
moss,
down air creaked with stars,
old Rocks moldering wainscot
both sweet and dried.
Sea,
I think a little pot with
green and weed.

Seeing Humming Tiger

Hair white as bleached sugar, height high as geeked toddler, I am young but
you will see me coming.
I smother you, filling you with the stares that you are destined to
give me, paint me, color.
Fur striped, black, grown tall several feet, I am clarity only animated cloning.
Humming tiger designing itself multiple and cerebral, I know you are looking.
Hair accented with purple, beak full of insect, I am young but
I rip through attacking:
You swallow my color in small bits before it can run away,
destroy my starvation.
My chest goes wild as gunpowder, while nothing can outdo my breath,
dazzle, dazzle jolting,
Hummingbird equipped for the long haul, I am a strong machine true,
I know you are viewing.

Turtle

I became a turtle when I did not know the answer
in elementary school, when I had to perform in gym
class,
in middle school when the teacher scolded me, when
they laughed,
in high school, when taking a test, in college when the
professor
called on me and for a few moments appeared to be just
slow
or deaf. I became a deaf dog when my friend poured
milk
on top of my head in the cafeteria while everyone
looked on and a bully proclaimed, I was sweet, in such
hate.

I was still a turtle when I realized I had to accept being
me
or gay. I became a gay human the day my mom lovingly
sent
me to school wearing tight jeans as a kid, I'm sure she
thought

it was cute but my peers assumed it was my attempt to stand out.

I was being me, but they were deaf and neither did they see me.

Perhaps, they saw a fuzzy turtle with table light chirp but what they failed to construct in their mind is that I was about

to fly through walls punctuation free and living my dreams.

Signed,

Turtle who became the tiger, who became the hummingbird, who

always saw useless trees. I am forever free.

Got the Dream

Your birthday is tomorrow, and I will not sleep,
I want to be up and ready to borrow the
known air of which I will breathe as I purchase your
gift of which I forgot last year, forgot out of
powerful distractions, forgot because I am
lame, (as you would say) forgot as I sought romance.
The gift will be purple your favorite color and
might just be a special kind of make-up (blocking
nothing on your face) of course.
Your cheekbones are sexy although, I know you do
not treasure them, your well aligned teeth, I know you
love maintaining them, I know you love whitening,
I know because they show when you talk,
but this make-up will help make your whites so dreamy,
I know you will so surely love it.

Got the Mic

You say hello, rejoices in the many smiles and snaps.
Your poetry will be shot out of cannon in seconds
and you got the dreaded mic.
The girl comes forth in your tale of why she is sad at the
moment. You excuse her to bring in the other girl whom
she somewhat envies. Then the boy barges in
announced by
only his testosterone, yet they all play their role, play
their role, roll through the motions, they become a
splendid poem
so, you decide to end things, since the crowd loves you
and you
want to leave them wanting more.
The curtains close, you bow out respectfully, yet in a
slight manner, you say goodbye; where to find your
books, they turn
off the mic, you are all done.

Be careful not to drop this mic.

Got the Document

We just want you to sign this document after reading these pages online, we just expect you to be fast, yet accurate and complete a survey on our company afterwards, got the document? I emailed you hours ago, please check your spam folder, did you get it, oh great.

Got the Phone Call

I eventually say how glad I am that you called, how we just never get to spend enough time together. You mention that
you are getting married and would like for me to be there,
I cannot, not for any reason other than I am
just upset with you, you love to leave me out of the loop,
that really puts me in a bad mood, our relationship suffers just because of it.
There comes a wide silence and they become more frequent, then
you interject with the fact (or supposed fact)
that you need to use the bathroom and take care of some things. Soured I say okay and hangs up phone.

Soured

I have accepted that when my generation
gets older, then so will the older ones that came
before ours of course, I am with book fearsomely
reading the minutes away as the seconds on
the microwave counts down. My food will be ready
soon but if I do not eat soon, it just might get
soured.

A staff member at my apartment complex came
over and changed something that had completed its
run. The staff member new exactly where to go,
the layout of our rooms is all the same pretty
much.

I wish I had the ability to improve
our bodies to the degree that I deemed worthy,
then might generations of people pause it all
perhaps, we are already slowing our great
graduation day unto a better newer
time.

Married

It is a whole new ballgame,
there's little time for my friends
and non-immediate fam.
I do not have space for your
Whispers and rumors oh child,
and leave that mess at the door
if you are lucky enough
to be invited over.
My spouse treats me well and makes
good money, I know you want
to know. My kids are under
the age of two, I started
late. I keep up the house, we
keep up house, we are a team.

Got the Message

Today we had an argument.
Today I question if my life
will split.
Today I triple my daily
prayers, meditations and
affirmations to get there.
Today I am feeling so down,
"Yeah man, I heard you the first time".
Today you threw a bowl at me,
today I am going to call
the police.
Today we went to the courthouse.
Today you cursed out the tall judge.
"Do not try to contact me for
Now",
I say hoping you got my drift.

My Drift

I am daydreaming as I look out the window in Math
class.
I am perplexed by the springtime beauty
outside the narrow bright glass as I marvel and insult my
teacher all at once. What could be out that window
that was just
better than his lesson.

Shimmering Night Water

At the water, at night.
My dreams come alive. Can you feel it?
Can you see it? The water, so serene,
so beautiful with everything, even the
air so light, it competes with this
light. All the while, I am here, contesting
nothing, because everything is right at this
very moment. Can you see the water, so
beautiful. This is my friendly place. Look
at the water, so beautiful. The water is
alone with only me to comfort it, and
although, I am only one person. The
water has the sky, the grass and the
trees. Oh, forget these cars that drive by
so blindly, they zoom by with them
polluting smoke, oh so in a hurry ego,
but I have you, and only you, all to
myself. I have you and only you all to
myself. Say it once more, I have you
and only you all to myself.

Part 2

I can be as stingy as the night,
I can be as giving as the grass,
I can be as careful as the house,
I can be as free as the horses
partner and the horse's friend.
What say you? What do you
have for me on this very night
with these night birds squealing
for comfort. What say you, what
say you most. Do you believe in
me, do you believe in the lights,
do you believe in that one
single star. I do not know,
perhaps you cannot see it.
Perhaps you cannot see my
Face. Can you see these
bicycles, all cluttered together
as if they are freezing from the
night cold, under this shed for
protection. Yes, I see you, I see
all of you, and you are beautiful
also just like the water

shimmering in the night, just like
the water also shimmering in the
night, just like the water
shimmering in the night.

Washed

For the show Color Splash that aired on HGTV

Thank you, David, I was feeling a bit washed when I turned on
the TV and found your track of consciousness and boy was my
mind following your brand new and unwashed clothes bound to my eyes,
tumbling drying out any potential distractions and blah
unimportantly up against David Bromstad's shooting voice.
You made a big statement just with your tame yet wild presence and
personality and bang your talent, you captivate me.

Thank you for starting your career yet giving an implosion
of angular ideas and huge hues, thank you so much guy,
you have ignited a combination of color and home.
Your friendly antics greeting; presenting people with choices

made my days and keeps me tuned in to your future endeavors.

I am in gear for interesting people who want to splash their home with your warmth and coolness since everything you do makes
sense.

I like the way you use accessories to update a room,
I like even the designs on your skin, since we know you will
Continuously add to them throughout the years yes, David.
I like your drive and I am living for everything, you.

Fill in that Green

I see chlorophyll in that green sheen
bringing me peace with leaves.

I see beating things deep and pristine,
unforeseen keys, no age,
the weeks freely into the future.

I see trees leaving me,
bringing me tea and my destiny.

I see seeming valleys
observing mysteries and living
months cautiously open.

I see the fields golden and streaming,
chlorophyll in that green.

I Am not a Victim – Affirmation

I am strong, needlessly,
I have healed from false threats, I am healed.
I am hammering back negativity
with my infinite strength.
I am always encompassing like a speeding sun,
you had better watch out,
I am dry ice to your picnic cooler,
this is not a walk in the park,
I speak from my soul; I bind any negative
energies sent my way, like dust afraid of my
giant tires now let us review, *(repeat once)*.

I Am Protected – Affirmation/ Song/Poem

<u>In my singing voice:</u> *I am protected, I am protected, when everything*
is going down, I stand still and I remember that I am protected.
<u>In my speaking voice:</u> I am protected, I am magnificent, when everything
is going down, I stand still and I remember, that I am protected.
My heart beats with fire and when my heart stops everything comes
back to me, I am protected. My blood is pumping of the waters and when
water stops, everything stops just the same, I am protected.
My skin crumples like the earth and when my skin stops, there is
Nothing but black and stars, I am protected. My breath is of windy air
And when the wind goes home, I will stop and remember that I am still

protected. The hot flames from your best stove will never beat the fire of this
heart for I know, and I remember that I am forever protected.

Me While Listening to The Verve "Bittersweet Symphony"

Hand reaches for honey laced cashews,
Hand shuffles the double crunch cheddar chips,
Hand squeezes the new glazing bottle of water.
I am hearing so much more sweet than bitter,
I am enjoying the sounds coming from the speaker,
and the world feels tranquil, my world sounds calm,
and I feel like walking down the street knocking
people over, without saying excuse me or I am sorry
people, I did not mean it. I am in my otherwise gloomy
room but the music announces my upbeat love of my
room right now. All is serene, the people in my life
will not dare make me upset, I do things that keep my
life
positive which means there actually is no bumping into
anyone
but I can bump up the volume on my headphones
and no one can say anything about it.
I am touring the heavens, I will look to replicate this
feeling,
hand reaches eventually for the off button.

Hand reaches to turn music back on, now we are listening to
Coldplay "Fix You". I am cool because the air conditioner is
running and it is helping to dissipate the heat, and fix me,
how befitting.

Me While Watching Fatboy Slim "Praise You"

Of course, my favorite is the lady with the short black hair,

being propelled through the air, her variations of blue clothing,

her jiggles all the while keeping a straight face, even her white

sneakers beneath her slightly elevated pants. In the video you

seem like a down to earth person or just someone I would not

run away from, you seem like you make your friends and family

laugh with your unconventional sense of humor which actually

would match me sometimes.

You Are a Different Kind of Sweet

I am on my tippy toes floating toward your essence. Nothing seems to compare to your stare (as if I needy your assistance). I flow to you like water in a stream or river. My thirst for you is now hidden because I have learned how to stealthily steal pictures of your face with my eyes while you are moving. I meet you like an intersecting gun, whereas it is almost a right angle and almost prepared to break and shoot its bullet for just only to obtain your attention. Again, I am on my tippy toes dancing to your charisma, skating to your charm, satisfied knowing that I will eventually have a better version of you, a one just for me.

Crystalline Icicles

I have sat with icicles,
yes, crystalline and the
opposite of mirrors, deep,
clear and fulfilled, showing
me continental streams, sharp
and smooth like awkward darts,
rolling fingers. I have given watery
dirt to a tongue before. I have provided
the rocky slopes its sheen and frozen fire.

I Have Learned that Some Humans Need Apologies

Some of us find apologies to be like the oxygen in a room at our
birthday parties, and if you find out that you are the one who has
to apologize you feel like you would rather not wear that ugly
dress. Some of us are valiant, some of us are valiant in other things,
some of us fear doing the very thing that we expect from others.
Some of us not only play the victim but we keep count of all the
Wrongs that have been done to us as if that scores you points with
the heavens, whereas instead it is better to keep track of what you
do for others.

Watered Down Coffee

Are you mad?
You threw up on my carpet.
You proclaimed that it was only
a little bit but you did not
clean up after yourself.

If this day to turn cold
I will proclaim that I have
Lived and I have experienced
what I needed to complete
my purpose here.

I hear the rain soaking
the soil outside and I
remembered that I need
a new light bulb for the
kitchen.

Forgive Me

Forgive me and let us begin the cycle of starting anew, recuperating from whatever those before us have done. Recuperating from whatever I have done or have not done
to you. I forgive you also, for if you have slighted me in any
way, I am free of it.
I am choosing to let this go.

Where do We Begin from Here?

We begin from here.
Leaving out the trauma and hurtful goodbyes.
We progress, we begin anew creating our own stories
so beautifully better than anything they could throw
at us,
even the ones you love or are supposed to love, trust.
We plant new seeds of caramel and honey and toss the
immature ones that look like milk and the spoiled ones
that
look like over-seasoned eggs.
We put our socks on one foot at a time, eat an
invigorating
breakfast. March with the penguins, scour with the
dogs
our next journey. We begin from here, wherever you
need to go.

Crisp Grilled Shade

I know something of a crisp grilled shade.
The birds forgot to eat their morning.
The ants forgot to sleep under the leaf.
The white clouds forgot to turn blue.
The trees forgot to do what they do.
I know something of a crisp grilled shade.
I know something of a crisp grilled shade.
I know something of a crisp grilled honey
on my pancakes, that I am eating in front
of you and then I walk outside my doors
into the sun as I pace myself, as I breathe,
as I sing, and as I hope that I will have my
crisp grilled honey tomorrow on my
pancakes in front of you.

Art Is

Art is easy, complicated, simple, refined,
rough, bold, golden, playing in a field
with another, good hands, broad
strokes, dancing in the stove, moving
like a grove, answers in time, solutions
for mine, vitamins at the right day,
wonders at night, tracks, freight,
measurements and chemistry.

Art is all the things I never did rolled
into one, all my dear hopes inside my
lungs. It helps me through my home
like a caretaker. Art is weary,
drenched, tears, revisited, illustrations,
loneliness, resumes, pictures, a cover,
ancient, rings on my finger, color on
my skin, closure and just about
everything.

Droopy Silence (version 2)

Droopy silence. Are you coming to save me?
I can hear you in the trees, yes, I can but actually
no, I cannot.

Droopy silence. Is this your world of luck, chance,
a world of pretentious surprises. I am here
benefiting from your wondrous applause, which
is silence tickling my ears, giving me something
to do and that is all I need right now.

Droopy silence. Do me a favor and get this message
the first time. I want to go to the shimmering night
water in the crisp grilled shade, below the droopy
silence.

Recipe to Make Water

And you will need one gallon of flowing art
three cups of exploding yet droopy wind
one tablespoon of a transcending moon
with a hint of orange sun.
A sprinkle of shoetree
And a blast of
torrential
grace.

The Tree that Grew
from the Pond

The tree thar grew from the pond,
I see you even though you are clear.

And the forest a sheer green in my mind.
And the trombone a loud tea for the sky.
And the parade a marching heap staring blind.
And me full of rich Indian, Honeybell rivers
trying select almond milk to harmonize with.

Renegade

We met at the thoughtful music box.
We paragraphed mutual days in mail.
We laid our cement away from them.
We slept at the thoughtful music box.
We shared minutes without our coffee.
We built our own cities more loyally sung.
We are renegades, not from their voice.
We are a reference of reviews dictating us through.

My Quotes

"Do not be bossy to people, let the Universe do it, for even if they go unnoticed, justice does not."

"You never know what you mean to another person."

"I look to be concerned with what I do, rather than what has been done to me."

"I am choosing to let this go."

Acknowledgments

Thank you:

Button Poetry, for being a vehicle extending poetry into the stratosphere, I am with you. My parents for giving me a firm enough foundation. My grandparents for being leaders of my family. To every assistant, editor, sponsor, contributor and reader. Tom Proietti, when I made discoveries in your class it meant so much. Alice Pratt, the music teacher who inspired one of my previous poems, thanks. Robert Harris, for your encouraging talks in the military. Richard Williams, for the encouragement in the military. Marie Ready, for being there. Noah Manny, for your smile and efforts. Krista Guererro, for listening. Navneet K. Atwal. Alexa Andewelt. Adam Epstein. Michele Ledoux-Pascucci. Kerry Rae Creasy, for your wonderful feedback. Julie Rattley, for being awesome. Tasha L. Harris, for being your extraordinary self. Brenna Twohy, for being so brave. Sarah Kay, for letting your voice shine. Dr. Maya Angelou, for being in a lane all by yourself, in my eyes. My brother for teaching me things and being receptive.

My sister, for taking care of business and being an awesome mother. Most importantly, myself Corporal Chaston D. Marshall a.k.a. Kasey C. Jones. So many people for which if I included your names and exactly how you have benefitted me, my Acknowledgments page would be so much better but dreadfully long but thank you.

Printed in the United States
by Baker & Taylor Publisher Services